CUTTING GHOSTS

HEATHER JACOBS

Cutting Ghosts

Heather Jacobs

Published by Trellis Publishing, 2021.

CUTTING GHOSTS

First edition. July 5, 2021.

ISBN: 979-8224266616

Written by Heather Jacobs.

Shannon Taylor had stood in the kitchen of her two-bed apartment, eyes clenched shut and hands gripping the work surface as if her life depended on it, her knuckles white, her hand and arm muscles a solid mass of stone. Between pursed lips, her teeth had ground together as if to crush away the image that powered through her brain. She had felt no pain, just a rush of adrenalin that crashed through her body. It had not been the first time that this had happened, but it was the first time that it had happened like this. Fortunately, the episode had been a short one, fortunate because in the master bedroom her boyfriend was still asleep.

It had been two o'clock in the morning and she had awoken from a disturbed sleep, sweat beading over every inch of her body, her nightgown drenched and clinging. Creeping from the bed so as not to wake David, she had made her way to the kitchen to get a long drink of water. She had just managed to fill the glass and place it on the work surface before the image struck.

She saw a young woman, barefoot, shoes lost in her desperate dash to cross the open field towards a house and safety. Every few seconds she glanced behind her to see the figure of a man gaining on her, his hand clutched a butcher's knife, his eyes gleamed red, his mouth curled in a mask of hatred, spittle flowing from his lips like a rabid dog. The woman tried to run faster, arms pumping, heart pounding but she was losing the race.

The distance to the house grew shorter, safety came closer. She called, she screamed but no one answered, no light flicked on. She was left abandoned in the semi-darkness of moon filled night.

She could hear his footfalls, dampened as they were by the soft grass beneath their feet. he was closer now and there was nowhere left to run. She had begun to cry, tears washing down her reddening cheeks, leaving smudged tracks through her make-up.

Then she felt it, the blade went deep into her left shoulder causing her to stumble, to fall. She lay face down, spread-eagle upon the earth, its pungent aroma invaded her mouth and nose. He was standing above her, legs spread to each side of her body, knife poised.

All at once he sat upon her legs, pinning them, and began to stab and slash. She felt her back, her shoulders, her spine, her lungs, her heart, torn to shreds in the frenzy of his attack. She saw the life she knew, the hopes and plans that she had, ripped from her thrashing, twisting frame before blackness overcame her and she remained still.

Though the woman was so obviously dead, the attacker was not finished with her. In her dream state, Shannon had seen him pull back the strands of bloodied blonde hair and; with neat, swift strokes, cut the ears from the lifeless head, the pendant earrings still attached.

Shannon saw him stand over his victim, a satisfied gleam in his eyes, his mouth now smirking as he looked towards the moon as if to drink in the pale light that cascaded onto the scene. Then he raised his arms aloft and laughed, loud, deep and uncaring.

Shannon had awoken then, coming back to a present that seemed alien in its peaceful normalcy. In her terror, her bladder had vacated itself and she stood in a pool of liquid slowly spreading across the floor. All was quiet. No sound came from the bedroom. She knew then she must have been silent throughout the whole episode. Quickly she had moved to clear up the mess, pull a clean gown from the chest of draws and take a shower to remove the smell of sweat and fear.

When she returned to the bed she shared with David, she had found, thankfully, he was still sound asleep. The side where she had lain, however, was still damp and she could not bring herself to lay there again. Opening the closet she pulled down a blanket and went to stretch out on the sofa in the sitting room. For the rest of the night, filled with the pale glow of a full moon, she lay between waking and sleeping, her body desperate for the rest, her mind fearful of what it would see if she allowed Hypnos to have his way.

Over breakfast the next day she and David had talked. Not about her episode, but about their relationship. She was torn between wanting to see more of him and fearing that she might scare him away if she appeared to clingy. Previous relationships had failed, at least in her mind, because she had been eager to invest more in them than her partner at the time had been. She had recognized the signs in herself and struggled to be cautious.

They had met a little more than a month before and, while they seemed to be a perfect fit for each other, Shannon wanted to be sure. David had stayed with her several times since they met and each time was better than the one before. It was only natural, she had told herself, that she should want to spend more time with him. Nevertheless, she was determined to move at his pace if it meant that the relationship would grow.

After they had finished eating, David had said he had to go and then he had taken her in a great bear hug, his massive frame and long arms wrapping around her. In the euphoria of the moment, Shannon had giggled like a school girl, the fears of the previous night lost in the safety of his embrace. He then kissed her and left her alone. It would be days before she had the opportunity to see him again.

In the loneliness of her apartment images from her dream flashed back, making her feel uneasy. She pushed them aside, a nightmare from which she had now awoken. The next hour was taken up with cleaning the apartment and stripping the bed. If David had noticed the dampness of the sheet he had said nothing. Once the washer-dryer was loaded, the bed remade and the place straightened, Shannon dressed and headed for the mall. There had been errands that needed to be taken care of and she wanted to buy a gift for David. There was no special occasion, she wanted to because she could. She would not give him the gift straight away, better to surprise him later.

Crossing the main road, Shannon had slipped down a side street that she knew would bring her out by the mall. On her way, she passed a small shop devoted to the occult. She had passed it many times but today, for reasons that she could not identify, she stopped and stared at the doorway, hidden in shadows of a sun-filled morning. Pulled by an unseen force, Shannon had found herself standing, looking through the large window at the paraphernalia that was on display. Suddenly she became aware of the owner staring back at her, dark curls framing a pale, oval face. Her eyes appeared black but, as they caught the light, Shannon could see they were the deepest purple.

Without realizing it, Shannon had taken a step back. She was standing in the middle of the alley watching a disembodied hand beckon her to enter. As foolish as it may have appeared, Shannon had not felt threatened, so she had stepped into the gloom of the shop, the only light being that which crept in from the street.

'You have had many, haven't you,' the owner had said. She was dressed in a black skirt and top, in keeping with the atmosphere of the place.

'I'm sorry,' Shannon said, confused.

'Dreams, you have had many of them.'

'I... well... yes, I suppose I have.'

'They are mot dreams, my dear,' the owner had whispered, staring intently.

It was only then that Shannon realized that the woman was considerably older than she had first thought. Maybe it was a trick of the light, but she appeared to have more wrinkles about her eyes and mouth than she appeared to have when Shannon saw her through the window.

Shannon smiled nervously, 'if they are not dreams, then what are they?'

'Premonitions.' The word had hung like the sword of Damocles in the oppressive silence of the shop. A silence that seemed to drag on and on.

'You need to trust them,' the owner went on, 'though you clearly do not know it yet, the things you see will happen... All of them!'

Shannon had the sudden urge to get clear. She almost ran from the gloomy silence of the shop. Back in the street, she had turned to look back through the shop window but the owner was nowhere to be seen. At that moment Shannon needed a coffee. Picking up the pace, she had almost run to the mall and the small coffee shop just inside the entrance. Shannon had ordered a cappuccino and found a seat away from the other patrons. The shop owner's words had unsettled her. If what she had said was true, then some poor, unfortunate young woman was going to lose her life. But when? Where?

That night Shannon had the same experience. She saw the same woman, the same man, the same scene. It played out through her mind as if it were a rerun of a slasher movie; every detail, every act, every word, perfect in its performance and delivery. She had awoken to another sweat covered body, clammy gown and aching muscles where the tension in them had forced her body into a rigid mass. The only difference was that she was still in bed, alone.

Lying there, shivering in the dampness of her sheets, Shannon recalled the words of the shop owner; the things you see will happen... All of them! Slowly she had pulled herself from the bed, thrown off her nightgown and padded naked through to the kitchen. She had poured herself a glass of water, drank a few sips, placed the glass on the counter and begun to cry. Somewhere through the flood of tears, a rational strand had found a footing in her brain. Logic demanded that she grasp hold and see where it led.

Following her line of reason, she had explored the premonition, content for the moment to accept the shop owner's assessment of what was happening to her. As she played out the scene she focused her mind on the background and not the people. As if through a fog, a realization began to materialize. She was aware where this field was. She had knowledge of the house. The reason no one heard the woman cry out, or come to her aid was because the place had been abandoned for years. No one lived there. It was isolated from the town so how had the woman gotten there? Nothing in her premonition gave an answer to this question.

The more she had thought about what had happened, the more logic crept in. None of what she had heard or experienced made sense. No one in her family had ever claimed to be psychic, Shannon would not claim it for herself. The whole idea had become ludicrous in her mind. A fanciful journey incorporating familiar places and stereotype people, and almost given credibility by the words given in a strange shop by a stranger woman. What she was experiencing, Shannon had concluded, was a bout of night terrors. She had had them as a child and knew that in time they would dissipate.

She had stood a few moments longer, staring at the glass on the counter. The light coming in through the window was the fading light from a waning moon. Shannon had breathed a deep sigh then. Calmer now, she had made her way back to bed. She had not climbed between the sheets but lay upon the bed and dragged the duvet around herself. Cocooned in softness, she drifted back to sleep.

She was awoken by the shrill ringing of the phone be the bed. Dazed she had grabbed for the received and missed. She had tried again and managed to get a firm hold. Putting it to her ear she caught the deep, dulcet tones of David. He had said that he was going to be away for a little while as the company was sending him up the country to deal with a distribution issue. He had taken the time to assured her that he would call on his return. It was with a great deal of disappointment that she replaced the receiver. She had hoped to see him again that coming weekend, the last before her leave was up and she would have to return to work.

To get over her disappointment she decided that a bout of retail therapy was in order. Once showered and dressed, Shannon headed for the shops. Without being aware she had avoided the alleyway where the occult shop was situated, taking a much longer route to the mall. On the way she had indulged in a considerable amount of window shopping, making mental notes of things that she liked for possible purchase later, either that day or better still, when David was around to accompany her. She had to admit that one of the things she liked about him was the fact that he was not like other men she had known. David actually enjoyed shopping with her.

It was in a department store, amongst the women's fashions that Shannon first saw her. The blonde hair, pendant earrings, clothes. She was exactly as she had appeared in Shannon's night terrors. Instinctively, Shannon cast about. It took a little time but she found him. He was lurking in another section of the store, but he never took his eyes off the blonde woman. He moved when she moved, stopped when she stopped. To anyone paying attention, like Shannon, it appeared that he was stalking the blonde. Shannon had looked back to where his prey still moved unaware through the clothing lines. She was distracted, giggling and chatting with a friend as they held up various outfits for scrutiny, neither aware of the danger just feet away.

Shannon had to do something, anything. Almost without thinking she had pulled her mobile from her purse and snapped both predator and prey. Now what? How could she warn this woman of what was going to happen? Did she even know when it would happen? A thought had come to her then. In her night terrors the moon had been full, but last night it was on the wane. There was time, but precious little of it.

Rushing from the store she had made her way to the nearest police station. The man must surely have a record. If she could get the police to listen then maybe, just maybe, the blonde woman's fate would be changed.

Shannon had almost crashed through the door to the police station, such had been her desire to get them involved. Approaching the desk she had demanded to see a detective or someone in charge. When asked her business Shannon had blurted out that there was going to be a murder and they had to stop it. When she looked back on this moment years later she was going to have to admit that she seemed like a deranged lunatic. But at that moment time was everything and Shannon had none to waste.

She was led into an interview room where she was joined minutes later by a female detective. Shannon had explained everything; the night terrors, the meeting with the shop owner, the woman she had seen being murdered in her dreams and the man she claimed was going to do it. The detective had listened patiently, making notes as the interview progressed. Shannon even taken out her phone and showed the detective the pictures that she had taken.

The detective listened patiently, even looked at the pictures., took down a few more details then asked Shannon to wait. Shannon did wait. She waited for the best part of an hour before the detective returned. As calmly as she was able, the detective had informed Shannon that, as far as they could tell, the man in question was not wanted for anything and, given that he had not committed a crime yet, there was nothing they could do.

'But I've told you. You have to believe me,' Shannon had pleaded, 'in less than a month this man is going to kill this woman. He is stalking her right now, I've seen him.'

'Unless this woman makes a complaint, there is nothing we can do.' The detective had sounded sympathetic but it was clear that she was not going to take action. Shannon looked at her, all calm in the face of Shannon's own anguish. She must think I'm crazy, Shannon had considered.

She had left the station then, a riotous ball of disbelief, anger, concern and even dread. If no one else was going to take action, Shannon had concluded, then she was going to have to do so. She decided that she was going to find this woman and alert her. Maybe she could even get her to make a complaint. It might just scare the guy away. It was the only plan she could come up with at the time so it was going to have to do.

For the rest of that week and all through the weekend that she had hoped to spend with David, Shannon had searched all the department stores and shops in the town. Every day she went to the mall, feeling certain that the young woman would spend some time there. No matter where she went she could find no trace of either the potential victim or the culprit. Shannon hardly slept through those first few days, so it was no wonder that she was exhausted by the time she was due to return to work.

If she had had a good night's sleep that final night before work, Shannon might even have given up the search as a fool's errand. But she didn't. The night terrors came again, more vivid, more urgent than before as if knowing that the two people involved were real made it all the more inevitable. A sense of doomed impotence had settled over her during those days, yet still she spent time searching. Taking an unpaid leave of absence on the grounds that she had to care for a sick relative. Shannon was sure that, if the police did not believe her, her work colleagues would think she had lost the plot, especially if she told them the real reason for wanting time away.

Day after day the routine had become the same, a snatched breakfast before the sun had risen, throw on the first thing that came to hand and out of the door. While there had been an ounce of daylight, Shannon was combing the streets, lanes and alleyways of the town. She had taken to going into every shop, every store, every petrol station, every church, every office block in an effort to locate the blonde woman.

Failure to locate her at one place fuelled the fear that maybe she had just missed her or that she would turn up at the last place she had visited. Shannon had also taken to showing the picture that she had of the woman to everyone she met. At first, people were kind and as helpful as they could be, but as days turned into weeks they avoided her. Little by little Shannon was barred from bars and venues, shops and offices, eventually all places of business.

That was when she had taken to wandering the streets on a constant look out. Several times she thought that she had seen the person she was looking for, only to discover to her embarrassment that they were not. In a matter of days, Shannon had become the person she thought the attacker was, a stalker. In a matter of days, she had become a homeless person living on the streets. She still had her apartment but, she had reasoned, time spent there was time away from searching for the blonde woman.

She had lost weight too. Clothes that had been a perfect fit now hung from a frame that had become gaunt and thin. People that she knew, unable to comprehend what she had been doing and why, feared that she had become anorexic. To hide her physical appearance, Shannon took to wearing the most loose fitting garments she could find. Far from disguising her state, such outfits just served to make her look even more in need of help. Yet she had continued to refuse it.

Little by little, the life that she had led up to this point was stripped away. Even her longing for David had been lost. She had seen him once in the weeks that had followed the first-night terror. He hardly recognized her. This man she had wanted to be close too, spend more time with, build a relationship with, a man who was understanding, supportive and real couldn't understand her obsession and, because of this, their relationship became strained to the point of breaking. Eventually, he stopped calling and hadn't been around for more than a week.

And the night terrors became more frequent. Whereas she used to have maybe one a year, she was now having them within days of each other. Each time the terror had been the same one that had put her on her quest. The close the time got to the next full moon, the more frequent the terrors had become. Hope was fading, to be replaced by desperation and failure.

It had been raining heavily that morning Shannon went back to the occult shop. The streets were mostly deserted so there was little chance of the blonde woman or her stalker appearing. Visiting the shop made sense to Shannon at the time. If anyone was going to know where the blonde woman was it had to be the shop owner. Why she hadn't thought of it before escaped her but now that she had there was no preventing her bursting through the shop door the moment the open sign had been displayed.

'Where is she? Where can I find her?' Shannon had demanded.

'Where is who, my dear?' the owner had said.

'You know who. You know that I have these dreams, these premonitions... you told me so, the things you see will happen... all of them, you had said. You know so tell me!'

'I cannot see your dreams, your premonitions, I only know that you have a connection with a higher power,' the owner had said, 'but I can tell you this, whatever you see has already been decided by the gods and there is nothing that you or I can do about it. To try to interfere, to change the course of the path that the gods have set will end only in disaster for you.'

'I don't believe you,' Shannon had screamed, leaping forward, a ball of churning anger and frustration, 'you know and you have to tell me.'

Shannon had taken the woman by the throat as they had crashed backward. Landing amongst several baskets of items that had meant nothing to Shannon, the two women had struggled and fought. Eventually Shannon, for all her wiry frame, came out on top. She had the owner pinned to the floor, handfuls of her hair in her fists.

Shannon had lost all sense of reason in her anguished attempts to find the truth, banging the owners head against the floor repeatedly until she passed out, leaving Shannon panting heavily and wracked by sobs of frustration.

When reason had come back to Shannon, she feared that, in her frenzy, she had killed the owner, so she had left the premises as quickly as possible and before anyone might discover the body. Stepping out into the alleyway she had become drenched through in seconds.

For a time Shannon had stood letting the rain wash her clean. She had even turned her face towards the heavens to drink in the precipitation and plead with the gods, that she did not believe in, to help her. A realization dawned at that time. In her nightmare the sky was clear, there had been no rain, the ground dry. There would be no death that day. Shannon made her way home, a wraith to everyone she passed.

The apartment was warm, the bed inviting. She hadn't thought about what she would do next. She had simply collapsed onto the bedcovers and disappeared into a deep sleep.

The clock on the bedside table showed 8am when Shannon eventually opened her eyes. How long she had been out she had no way of knowing, but the rain had stopped. Sunlight had washed through her windows, casting a golden glow over everything. Shannon had eased herself from the bed and, through a long-established routine, had thrown herself into a hot shower. The soothing balm of the shower gel eased some of the aches and pains that she had felt. For some time she had stood there, letting the needles of spray cascade over every inch of her body. It rejuvenated her and it was what she had needed.

She had stepped out of the shower, wrapped a towel around her torso and looked into the mirror. The image that stared back was not one that she could have recognized. She had become a stranger, even to herself. She had wrapped a towel around her head then and made her way to the kitchen. As she passed through the sitting room she had glanced at the phone. Sixteen messages had been left but Shannon hadn't stopped to listen to any of them.

In the bedroom, she had dragged on clean clothes then gone to the kitchen to make coffee. The milk had gone off so she had drunk it black, staring at the familiar walls of her sanctuary. She was taking the time to reacquaint herself with her past, to reconnect with the woman she had once been.

Her eyes had fallen upon the wall calendar and she had stared at it for some time. there were no marking, no notes or cryptic messages, the kit was completely blank and Shannon realized that she had no idea of the date. Taking her coffee with her, she had gone to the sitting room, found the remote and called up a news channel on the TV. When she had found what she was looking for she had returned to the kitchen and scanned the calendar. A small circle in the top right corner of the date told her all that she needed to know.

Shannon had spent the rest of that day doing normal things. Cleaning the place up, washing, changing the bed sheets. She ate, watched TV, listened to her messages, though she did not return any of them. She stocked the fridge and wrote a note that explained everything in case her plans went awry.

As the sun went down, Shannon had picked up her car keys, a map, a torch and the only weapon she could find - a claw hammer that David had once used to hammer some nails into the walls to hang pictures on. She had hesitated briefly at the door to her apartment before closing it and making her way down to the car.

She had no trouble starting the vehicle for a change. Sometimes, if it is left to stand for a while, it could be the most awkward thing to get going. The journey had been easy enough, little traffic was abroad that night. When she had reached her destination, Shannon parked the car and sat waiting.

Time moved slow. The moon rose as she knew it would, bathing everything in an eerie glow. The scene that she had seen in her night terrors was exactly as she saw it then. It was the right place, even down to the abandoned house that she could just make out across the field.

Shannon was prepared. There was a calmness about her now that she knew what she must do. The only thing that troubled her was the knowledge that nowhere in her premonitions had she seen herself coming to the rescue. Was the occult woman telling the truth? Was everything already fixed? Was this a fool's errand? Whatever the answers were to those questions, she was committed and there would be no change of heart.

Saw the woman first. She broke cover from the trees off to Shannon's left, quickly followed by her pursuer. The woman was screaming and calling for help, the man just laughed. Shannon had gotten out of her car and began to her own pursuit.

The ground was a little uneven and Shannon had stumbled a few times, creating a wider gap between her and the figures in front.

Determined to prevent what was about to happen, she had forced herself to move quicker. Her heart had pounded faster, her breath had come in gasps but she had closed the gap.

At the point where she was sure she would make it a dip in the ground caused her to stumble again. By the time she had found her feet again it was all over. The blonde woman lay face down in the dirt and the man laughed maniacally at the moon. Shannon had screamed then.

The man did not stop to find out where the scream had come from. He took off across the field. Shannon, determined that he would not get away with his butchery, took off after him. Try as he might, the man could not shake her pursuit. At one point, down a partially lit alley, he had turned to confront her. She saw the bloody knife in one hand, the severed ears in the other. His face, contorted in an image of hate. His eyes were red too, bloodshot as if he had not slept in weeks. Then he had taken off again and Shannon kept up the pursuit.

Through a maze of alleyways, he thought he had lost her, but Shannon saw him duck into a single story run down structure, a broken chicken wire fence marking the boundary of the property. Knowing where he was allowed Shannon time to catch her breath. She had waited until her pulse was more regular, then she approached the house.

She didn't go to the front. Instead, she had slipped around to the back and peered in through the window. He was there, admiring his trophies, the blood congealing across the cuts. Her next move had to be carefully thought out, but before she could decide he had stepped out onto the porch and saw her instantly.

In an instant, the blade was in his hands. Shannon had not hesitated. Launching herself forward she swung the hammer with as much force as she could muster. He ducked and brought up the blade and caught Shannon in the left shoulder. It was not a deep cut but it stung and for a moment had thrown Shannon off balance. Falling from the porch she had rolled several times in the grass of the back yard. he came striding after her.

Shannon had risen to her feet just in time to see him lunge at her, the knife stretched out before him. She had managed to deflect his arm while, at the same time, swing the hammer in a long arch that brought the head of it smashing into his temple.

Like a felled ox he went to his knees, arms hanging limp. Shannon was not going to take chances. She raised the hammer and struck him again, and again, and again. Her breathing became labored, her arm aching. By the time she had finished, unable to lift the weight of the hammer anymore, his head was a bloody mass of pulp, his body - sitting back on its haunches - remained still and strangely upright, blood still pumping from broken veins and arteries.

Shannon had been covered in his blood. It ran in rivulets down her face and arms. It soaked into the fabric of her clothes and its metallic aroma had assaulted her nostrils. In this state she had sunk to her knees staring at a murderer murdered. She had wept then.

By the time the police had arrived in response to her call, the bloody mass that was once a man was covered in flies and other insects. Shannon had marveled at the speed with which nature was determined to clear up the mess. Police officers surrounded her and she had let herself be lifted bodily, her weapon removed from her fingers, and then cuffed.

As she was being led away Shannon saw the detective she had spoken to weeks ago. 'Check his left hand,' Shannon had said, 'they belong to a blonde woman whose body can be found in a field next to the old Carter farm.'

Just then a shout had come from the back door, 'detective, you have to see this.'

'Bring her,' the detective had said, why Shannon would never know.

They had manhandled her up onto the porch and through into the kitchen, then she had been led through to one of the bedrooms off the lounge. The room had been furnished with a series of cabinets and display cases. Each one was filled with exhibits. pairs of ears, arranged like butterflies were pinned to cards bearing names, ages of the contributors and the dates and places where they had been taken.

There must have been hundreds, arranged chronologically. In the cabinet to her left Shannon had seen pairs of ears from children as young as one month. To her right there was a display case with the ears of the elderly, the oldest being a hundred and one. They were all perfectly preserved, almost as if they had been cut from the head that very day.

'Release her,' the detective had ordered.

'But...' Shannon's officer escort hesitated.

'It's ok, release her.'

The officers had done as instructed and Shannon found herself staring into the face of the detective as she rubbed her wrists where the cuffs had bitten.

'Go home,' the detective had whispered, 'get yourself cleaned up. We have work to do and you don't belong here.' Then she had turned away. Shannon had moved towards the door but before she could pass through it the detective turned back to her. 'We will need a statement,' she had said, 'call into the station in the next day or two, would you... please.'

Shannon had nodded, then said, 'could I get a lift home. My car is parked near the Carter farm. I don't want to walk the streets looking like this.'

An officer was assigned and Shannon was escorted back to her apartment. She had spent a long while in the shower that night. Like Lady Macbeth she had scrubbed and scrubbed in an effort to erase the evidence of her crime but she knew even then that it would stay with her always. And while she scrubbed, one thought kept going through her mind. How could this man have done what he had and get away with it for so long?

the events of the past weeks caught up with her then. Shock and horror overwhelmed her and she had collapsed into a corner of the shower, weeping uncontrollably. That was where David had found her. He had broken down the door when he got no answer to his knocking.

Not having had any of his calls returned had caused him alarm but he had been unable to find out what was going on until this moment.

Ignoring the cascade of water, he had stepped into the shower, sat beside Shannon and held her tight while she shed herself of all of her pent up emotion. They remained that way for some time. Shannon knowing that she had a gift that could not be ignored, David knowing that he would take care of her.

BONUS STORY:

The portions at this restaurant were huge... that's why he liked to hang out outside at this hour. People were always throwing away half their plates.

That's still good eatin'.

Digging through the trash that had just been dumped had rewarded Spencer with a nice helping of salad and a sizeable piece of meat still hanging off the bone.

It's a good night.

Spencer gathered his coat around himself as the twilight breeze wafted through his greasy hair. A smell of cigar smoke and cognac drifted through the air and into his flaring, thirsty nostrils.

He had a small bottle with a couple precious shots of whiskey left. He'd been holding onto it for a long time- over a week. He didn't exactly know when he was going to need it, so he kept it safe.

Most nights he could find bottles with some liquor left in them.

The streets provide.

Spencer took his rewards and settled in next to the dumpster. He picked a small piece of lint from his meat and sank his teeth in.

Still kind of warm.

As he chewed, his eyes wandered over to the high-end restaurant across the street. He never checked their trash anymore... the portions were the size of a thumb, and cost more than a night in a warm hotel.

Rarely were there leftovers.

But something other than food and drink caught his eye.

Something familiar...

A woman was approaching the entrance to the restaurant, on the arm of a well-dressed, manicured gentleman. Spencer brought his own jagged, stained, tough fingernail up to his mouth to dig a piece of gristle out of his rotting teeth.

She had a bracelet on her left wrist.

Gold, sparkling with diamonds.

Vanessa loved diamonds.

No, Vanessa didn't love anything.

She needed diamonds... required them like she could reap sustenance from them.

Vanessa...

That name hadn't stabbed his mind in quite some time.

Spencer remembered when he couldn't go two minutes without thinking the name... and of the almost supernatural beauty attached to it.

Vanessa...

That can't be her. It can't be. It's just some rich broad with a similar bracelet.

Similar to the one I had made custom for her supple wrist...

The half-chewed chunk of meat fell from Spencer's lips as his mouth and eyes hung open.

He followed her shapely legs as she strolled along the carpeted path that led to the restaurant. He followed the course of her fitted dress along her waistline, and up the revealing lines of her back.

Everything he was seeing was familiar, even though he hadn't seen it in years.

But it can't be her.

It can't.

Spencer struggled to his feet. He took a couple tentative, wobbly steps toward the apparition across the street.

Just before entering the restaurant, she turned and spoke into her companion's ear.

Spencer could almost feel the line of her jaw against his fingertips.

Gold and diamonds hung elegantly from her ears. Her eyebrows swept up like the wings of a bat.

It's her.

Spencer's entire body broke out into shivering, chilling sweat. Goosebumps prickled his dirty skin.

It can't be her... but it is.

She's right across the street.

Spencer felt a spasm wrack his body and he doubled over. He vomited next to the dumpster, losing what little nutrition he had managed to ingest.

As he gagged, tears filled his eyes.

Memories, pictures, scenarios that he hadn't allowed himself to think about in a long time came flooding back into his swimmy mind.

He gnashed his teeth and clenched the sides of his head.

Vanessa...

The name filled him with equal parts longing and hatred.

She took it all.

She took everything... and everyone.

It's all her fault.

Spencer shook his head violently, trying to jar these thoughts out.

It's not her. It's just someone that looks like her.

He looked back across the street, just in time to see the front doors close as the woman and her man entered the building.

Yeah. Definitely wasn't her.

Spencer reached into his coat and dug around for his bottle.

Wait... we're saving that for a time when we need it.

We need it.

No. Not yet.

Spencer pulled his shaking hand from out of his coat and clenched it into a fist.

He had forgotten about his found meal entirely.

The brick wall of the alley felt cool and calm as he slumped against it, trying to wrestle his broken thoughts.

Was it her, or wasn't it?

What does it matter?

What are you gonna do if it is her?

Spencer felt his blood run a little colder.

Who was she with?

Who was the man whose arm she walked in on?

Was it... Brad?

Spencer's teeth clenched, his lips curled back in feral anger.

Brad... the little worm.

The weasel.

The rat.

It was his fault.

He took her.

And they took everything.

Spencer hadn't felt much in the way of emotion in a long time. Survival had a way of paring back anything that wasn't necessary, emotion being a big one.

But now, his bones rattled with anger... anger he hadn't felt since this all started... since his other life crumbled away.

It didn't crumble away, it was taken from me.

Stolen from me.

Spencer felt his brain throbbing. This was too much.

If I can see them, see that it's not who I'm thinking of, I'll be fine. I just need to see. I can get back to my life as long as I know it isn't them.

And if it is them...

It's not.

But we need to be sure.

Spencer pushed himself off the brick wall and stood upright, with effort.

The street seemed twenty lanes wide, instead of the two it actually was.

Spencer's heart raced as he swayed on the sidewalk. People passing by gave him dirty, disgusted looks, but he hardly noticed.

He took a deep, shuddering breath and took his first steps across the sidewalk, his pack slung over his shoulder. He stepped onto the street, barely registering the cars passing by and honking.

The restaurant loomed before him... its glass doors a gaping maw. Windows wrapped around the dining area, affording passersby a decent view of the interior.

He stepped carefully across the street, each step an effort. Finally, his feet landed on the sidewalk that led to the restaurant.

The doorman gave him a pitying yet uninviting glance then pretended not to see him.

Spencer tucked his chin into his chest and walked left, glancing through the windows.

This restaurant was packed, full of rich younger couples and groups. No families, no children, just people who wanted each other to see them here.

Spencer had two crumpled dollar bills in his coat pocket, along with three quarters, a half-dollar, three dimes, and two pennies. He'd held onto this money for almost a month, trying to add more, but the streets hadn't been raining money as of late.

He continued around the building, glancing into the windows whenever he felt he wouldn't be too conspicuous. So far, he saw no one he recognized.

Having walked a full side, he turned and went around the back of the restaurant. The smells of strange foods drifted out of the kitchen, mixed with the cigarette smoke of a cook taking a break. Spencer kept to the edge of the property, trying to look and act as if he were just someone passing through a shortcut.

Relief was starting to fill his mind and relax his pulse.

It wasn't her. She's not here, and life is good. Everything is exactly as it's supposed to be.

He turned around the last side of the building, looking in the window.

There she was.

Spencer stopped dead in his tracks. A small gasp escaped his parched throat.

She was sitting at a table, laughing behind her napkin.

She lowered it and he could see her full face.

Her silken, porcelain skin.

Her eyes sparkling like emeralds.

Her delicate, snake-like features.

Her perfectly placed hair.

Her red, razorblade smile.

Spencer stumbled back, the wind knocked out of him.

His heart pounded in his chest, trying to hammer its way out.

He felt exactly like he did when he first laid eyes on her so many years ago... like a scared, jealous, nervous schoolboy trying to get a girl to notice him.

And he was painfully aware of himself. How he looked... how he smelled... the wreck his life had become.

You could walk in there right now and she wouldn't even recognize you.

She wouldn't even look at me.

You would disgust her.

Spencer wished more than anything that he could be disgusted by her. But right now, he only felt longing and shame.

He stared at her through the crystal clear window. He watched her laugh, smile, nod, and talk as though life was just fine, not a series of disasters and heartache.

His eyes finally slipped across the table to see who it was she was having such a good time with.

Spencer's face changed as he glared at the man.

It is Brad.

Brad, Brad, Brad.

We remember him well, don't we?

Of course. The man was my partner.

It was our names on the side of the building.

Spencer watched as Brad made some joke involving his drink and a spoon, which had Vanessa giggling behind her napkin again.

She doesn't want anyone to see her laugh... might make her human.

Brad pushed his thousand-dollar cufflink back so he could look at the face of his ten-thousand dollar watch.

He was my best man.

Brad leaned across the table and kissed Vanessa on the cheek. Spencer felt his thin blood race.

He stole my life.

That should be ME sitting in that expensive restaurant, with too much money and not enough places to spend it all.

I should be with her...

Brad hailed their waiter over, who left a check on the pristine table. He placed one of surely hundreds of credit cards on the table and the waiter whisked it away.

Spencer absentmindedly fumbled with the loose change in his pocket.

Three dollars and fifty-seven cents... that's what my life is worth now.

Tears wanted to spill out of his eyes, but he forced them back. Sorrow, anger, shame and disgust battled for dominance in his mind.

His shaking hand went back in his coat for the bottle.

We need to save that, we don't know when we'll get more.

I need it. Now.

Spencer fumbled the bottle out, wrestled the cap off, and poured the remains down his aching throat. The burn filled every scratch, every pit in his esophagus as it traveled down into his decaying guts. Then, a warm flood of relief, like a cloud floating on a breeze...

I could take him out.

That thought felt a little unnatural, like it wasn't his usual inner voice talking. But it was soothing, too.

That little worm has never had to actually fight for anything. His idea of fighting is to make a phone call or send an email behind somebody's back. He's never had to physically defend himself.

We have.

We've learned how to survive.

Does Brad know how to survive?

And if Vanessa sees that he can't... if she sees his weaknesses...

Spencer refused to allow himself to complete that thought.

The waiter came back to the table with a slip for Brad to sign. He and Vanessa got up to leave.

Alright, they're coming. Time to move...

What? Move where?

If you're gonna do it, you have to do it now.

Do what?

Don't we want to see him afraid?

Spencer tried to think straight.

Scare him a little bit.

Yeah.

What's the harm in that?

Spencer made his way back to the front of the building, hiding back and peeking around the corner.

After several people entered and left, Vanessa and Brad came out.

Spencer could barely hear them talking.

"...really have to be tonight?" Brad was saying.

"I don't want to deal with it in the morning, do you? It'll just take you a minute."

"Right now, I just want to go home, slip under the covers with you, and..."

"Watch me not enjoy myself because I'm too concerned with what you should have taken care of down at the office?"

"...yeah. Okay. I guess I'm heading to the office. Can we still share a cab?"

"I guess. But drop me off first?"

"That's not exactly on the way."

"I'm tired."

"Fine."

The office... There was only one building they were referring to.

And Brad's gonna be there alone. After hours.

It's perfect.

Two blocks to the north, there was a bus stop.

That would take him right downtown, just a block away from the office.

Just to scare him a little bit... remind him of who I was... who he stole his life from.

What does it matter? That was a different life. I was a different person. I've learned to live a new life, I know how to survive. Why not just let the past be the past?

Spencer wanted that thought to be stronger, but it was weak. His other voice just chuckled.

Minutes later, the bus stop was just down the walk. Spencer was stumbling a little, his heavy clothes and pack weighing him down. The sun had descended behind the cityscape and the sky was darkening to a deep purple. People walked far out of their way to get around him, their eyes averted but stealing quick looks at his pathetic life. Spencer hardly noticed. He was walking with a sense of purpose, with a mission.

The bench at the bus stop was occupied by a strung out looking couple, leaning on each other for support. Spencer stood behind, mostly hidden by a poster display covered in flyers.

The bus would be here in about ten minutes, according to the schedule. The office building was only fifteen, twenty minutes from there.

Spencer hadn't ridden the bus in two, three years at least. He hadn't gotten inside a car for three years before that.

How long has it been? How long have we been living on the streets, trying to forget about the life we once had?

I don't even know, Spencer thought. It made him feel sad.

We're just running through ALL the emotions today, aren't we?

It was at least ten years. Spencer tried to remember what year it was now, and found it very difficult. He thought he remembered seeing a newspaper some days ago with a date printed on it. What had it said?

Spencer wrestled with his confused thoughts until the bus pulled up with a screech.

He waited until everyone else had gotten on or off, and made his way to the door.

"Two bucks," the driver said as Spencer climbed on.

Spencer almost gasped. The price had gone up since he last rode.

Two dollars... that would only leave him with one dollar and fifty-seven cents.

That's a hamburger from a fast-food joint. Or a small bottle of something cheap.

Is this really how we're going to spend this money? Is this little trip down memory lane really worth it?

Two dollars had never seemed more expensive.

"Are you getting on or not? That's two bucks, buddy."

Spencer nodded, fished the two wrinkled bills from his coat pocket and reluctantly handed them over. The driver took them with a sickened look and shoved them in the coffer.

"Well, find a seat already. Let's get moving."

Spencer kept his face down as he shuffled down the bus. The smell of disinfectant was strong, enough to make him aware of just how bad he smelled.

He tried to stay away from the others on the bus, but still got a lot of revolted looks. He found a seat away from the others and crawled into it.

Through the bus window, he could see the city passing by. The buildings grew taller and more congested, the streets packed full of cars and pedestrians.

Sitting here, Spencer felt incredibly tired. The booze was making his mind swimmy. He wanted nothing else than to just go home.

Home... that's a funny thought.

Where exactly is home?

Any alley away from all of this is just fine.

Homesick without a home... now that's irony.

The bus eventually stopped where Spencer needed it to, and he shuffled off in a hurry. He didn't like being around people, in their places, in their eyes, in their world. He was more comfortable in the world he had learned to live in.

Back out in the open air, on the street, he felt better. Clearer.

This end of the city was a lot busier than the side in which he usually stuck. The buildings reached high into the sky, traffic was thick and noisy. The air smelled like exhaust, cigarettes and the mingling aromas of industry and competition.

The office building was just a couple blocks away. Spencer set out.

He felt like he was on a quest, some journey to a faraway land. But it was really a trip back in time... he used to walk these streets every day.

He could remember how his tight, Italian loafers felt striking the pavement. He could remember his crisp suit bending the wind around him... the weight of the briefcase at the end of his arm, a case full of authority. He remembered feeling powerful, like a man in control.

Suddenly, it was there. Looming above him like the leg of God. The building was a tower of steel and glass, reflecting back the city from which it had taken so much.

Spencer gasped.

And in huge, severe letters on the front of the building, the words:

Laughlin and Mills Realty

Mills...

That's my name. Spencer Mills.

I didn't even remember my own name.

Spencer was surprised to see his name still on the building... after so many years he would've expected the name to change.

He followed the windows with his bloodshot eyes, floor after floor after floor, until he was at the top offices. There, in a window to the left, a light was burning bright.

That'll be Brad's office.

Spencer started for the front doors, like he was just walking into work.

Wait…

How are we going to get up there? It isn't like you can just walk into this place anymore.

Spencer peeked through the doors.

The security post was empty and all the lobby lights were off. It looked like everyone was gone, except for Spencer.

Perfect.

He tried the door.

Locked.

That'd just be too easy.

Alright, why don't we just wait for him out here?

No. He'll have a car pick him up, they'll see.

Ok. So are we scaling the building like a superhero?

No. But what about the fire escape?

…that might work.

Spencer hurried around to the alley. There, beyond the dumpsters, was the fire escape.

How do we get the ladder down?

I think we just jump up and grab it.

Spencer positioned himself beneath the ladder and hopped up and down a few times until he grabbed hold of the ladder. He hung for a moment, dangling, until the ladder broke free and slid down fast. Spencer fell off, landing on his back with a pained grunt.

Graceful.

Spencer got back to his feet and mounted the creaky ladder. He climbed up onto the first level of the fire escape and began to ascend the stairs.

What floor are we going to?

Well, it used to be the 17th floor. But any floor with a window or door open will do.

The fire escape felt rickety and slightly loose, but that could've just been his sloshy brain. He checked the windows on the way up, but found none open. He huffed and puffed as he ascended. This was more of a workout than he'd gotten in a long time. And it just kept going. He climbed and climbed until he was sweating heavily in his thick coat. The ground became tiny in the distance. He tried not to look down.

After climbing for an eternity, he finally found a window that had been left cracked. Gasping, panting, he pried the window open and stumbled in. He fell on the floor, gulping deep breaths.

He struggled out of his pack and big overcoat, trying to cool himself down. He felt like he was going to pass out.

Keep it together, Spence. We got work to do.

The small office was dark, lit by small points of light from computers and power supplies. Spencer's eyes adjusted to the dark as he slowly rose to his feet. Leaving his coat and pack by the open window, he slowly opened the door of the office.

The floor seemed empty. He could hear no one, just the hum of electricity.

Down the hall, he could see the green glow of an exit sign. Slowly, he crept out into the hall and toward the glow.

The elevators at the end of the hall were lit by a soft orange light. Spencer could see now that he had climbed to the 22nd floor. He pushed the button to call the elevator.

Spencer stood before the elevator doors, a ragged, hairy, mess of a man. His eyes burnt holes through the doors.

Brad, Brad, Brad...

We're gonna scare him good.

Ding.

Spencer walked into the elevator car, pushed the button for 17, and waited.

Five floors down, the doors opened, Spencer stepped out, and there was Brad.

Spencer's eyes widened.

Brad was walking toward the elevator, looking down at his phone. He almost walked right into Spencer before looking up.

Spencer's heart began to pound.

What the hell am I doing here?

Brad saw him and screamed a short little yip like a small dog. His body jerked back and he dropped his briefcase and phone.

"Hi, Brad!"

"Woah! Woah there! Who are you, buddy? You're not supposed to be in here."

"Yes I am. I am supposed to be here."

Spencer was angry.

His heart rate slowed, evened out. His vision became crystal clear.

He forgot how the anger used to power him.

Spencer closed his hand into a tight fist and smashed it into Brad's nose.

The pop echoed in the hallway and blood poured onto the reflective floor.

Brad stumbled back and clapped his hand over his broken nose. He slipped on the squeaky clean floor and fell on his ass.

Spencer stood above him, feeling strong, in control.

"What the hell, man? What'd you do that for?

"Do you know who I am?"

"No, I've never met you, man! You must have me mixed up with someone else."

"Brad Laughlin. That's you."

"Yeah, that's me, but..."

"It's been a few years, but you know me."

"I don't know you, man, I..."

"Look at me, Brad. You know me."

Brad looked. He looked at Spencer's leathery, weathered face, scraggly beard and greasy tousled hair. He had tears in his eyes.

"I swear I don't... I've never seen..."

Then recognition came over his face.

"My god, Spencer? Is that you?"

Spencer expected a great swell of pride as he heard his name spoken aloud. Instead, he felt only shame... shame at his failures, shame at his current state, shame at being recognized for the first time in years.

Shame that this man was still on top of the world and Spencer himself was indeed at the bottom.

"You did this to me! You made me into this!" Spencer screamed out.

Brad started to shuffle backwards along the floor, afraid.

"Spencer. Okay, I know you. I do. Look, I'm getting that you're upset, but..."

"Upset? You think I'm upset?"

Spencer advanced on Brad, who started shuffling away faster.

"Maybe upset isn't the right word..."

"Maybe it isn't, Brad. Maybe the right word is furious."

Spencer kicked Brad in the head with his ratty boot.

Brad yelped and collapsed on the floor, unconscious.

"Huh," Spencer said.

That was... fast.

I'm not done yet.

There were two doors on the wall beside the elevators.

One would lead to a mechanical room and the other would be the janitor's closet.

If I remember correctly, the janitor's closet is... this one!

Spencer flung open the door on the left.

Jackpot.

Spencer grabbed a roll of duct tape from the shelf to his left. There was a small desk to his right with a rolling chair. Spencer wheeled the chair out into the hall.

"Alright Brad, come on," Spencer said as he struggled to lift Brad from under the arms.

Eventually, with a fight, he got Brad in the chair. He ran duct tape over his arms, chest, and finally over the lap, securing him to the chair.

"Okay. Alright. You good? Yeah, you're good. Let's see what else we've got here."

Spencer pushed Brad along the tiled floor, wheeling him past offices and desks. The layout of the building was a little different in the dark, but everything was coming right back to him.

Before he knew it, he was standing in front of the big doors... the grand room, where almost all the real business was done. Spencer turned the knob and shoved Brad through.

Spencer flicked the switch on.

Harsh white light flooded the room.

Wow... it got bigger.

The room was, of course, the same size as it always was. But Spencer felt so small now, looking down the length of the huge table. He ran his hand along the tops of the chairs as he slowly walked down the room. Millions of dollars had been negotiated over this very piece of wood.

Spencer stood behind the head of the table, looking down across the room. He used to stand here, just like this, when he was about to deliver what he felt to be a particularly important speech.

Wait a second...

Spencer spun on his heel.

Hoo, baby!

The liquor cabinet was still there... oak, shiny, beautiful...

Spencer flung the cabinet open and cried out in delight.

Top shelf booze.

Lots of it.

And there, on the top, top shelf...

Glenlivet.

The world's finest single-malt scotch.

Holy mother of god.

Spencer took down the bottle with a shaking, reverent hand. It was almost entirely full.

He slowly unscrewed the cap.

The aroma drifted lazily up to his sore, red nostrils.

His mind drooled.

He grabbed a crystal glass from the cabinet and poured three fingers in.

He swished the liquid around the glass under his nose, breathing in the heady fumes.

He brought the glass to his lips, took a sip. Then he upended the glass in one swift, practiced shot.

The fires of heaven burned along his throat and settled in his belly, warm and comforting. Safe.

For a brief, blissful moment, it was twelve or thirteen years ago. He was working late, closing up a huge deal as usual. He was having a drink alone, hundreds of feet above the city... the city he had helped create.

Spencer closed his eyes and let the liquor do its work.

He could smell the wood polish from the gigantic table. He could feel his starched, pressed shirt... his fitted trousers and suspenders... his two-hundred dollar haircut.

Then Brad began to struggle.

Spencer's eyes sprung open.

Oh man, what have I done?

Brad was fighting against the duct tape, trying to free himself.

Alright, that's enough. I'm getting out of here.

We haven't heard him say he's sorry.

Who cares? None of this matters...

Yes it does.

It matters.

This should all be ours.

Spencer grabbed the bottle of Glenlivet and walked over to Brad. Taking a swig from the bottle, he ripped the duct tape from Brad's mouth.

"AHH!! Ouch!"

"Brad, Brad, Brad. It's been a long time, hasn't it?"

"Spencer. Look. Whatever you're planning on doing, there's a better way. Please let's just talk, alright? Do you wanna talk about it?"

Brad was talking fast, babbling between gasps. Spencer found himself enjoying the scene. He took another swig from the bottle.

"You're pissed off. I can see that. But look, it wasn't my fault. It was all her idea. I really just played along with what was already happening. Business right, ya know?"

Spencer took another drink and said nothing.

"Please just think for a second. You don't wanna kill me. I can get you money. I can get you whatever you want, really. Just please stop this and don't kill me man I just don't wanna..."

Spencer smacked him, just hard enough to shut him up.

"Kill you? I don't think I was planning on that. You're pretty sick, Brad."

Spencer took another, big gulp.

"Or maybe I was. I don't really know, to be honest."

Spencer started laughing. Brad cringed.

"I could kill you. The past few years have taught me a lot about survival."

Spencer pulled the chair out nearest Brad and sat down.

"I'll tell you a little secret Brad. You wanna hear a secret?"

Brad nodded emphatically.

"You wouldn't be the first person I've killed."

Brad began to whimper.

"The streets provide. But sometimes the streets can be tough, too."

Spencer took a big gulp, some of which spilled out of the sides of his mouth and into his beard.

"I learned to be tough too. I learned to be one tough sonofabitch." Spencer felt swimmy, but still powerful.

He set the bottle on the huge table and ran his hand along the surface, feeling the smooth wood.

"We ruined some lives over this table, didn't we? We took a lot of money. A whole lotta money."

"Spencer. Look. I get what you're saying. We messed up your life pretty good. And I'm really sorry about that..."

Spencer looked at Brad.

"What was that?"

"I... I'm really sorry. I know that doesn't begin to make up for what we did, but..."

He said he's sorry.

So... do we feel better?

Actually... no.

Not even a little.

Spencer grabbed the bottle again and drank deep. Booze splashed down his chest.

"We'll see who's sorry. Let's go on up to the roof, whaddaya say?"

"No, we don't need to do that, let's just talk this out..."

Spencer put the duct tape back on Brad's mouth. It didn't stick as well and Brad was shouting against it, but it was more for effect than anything else.

He grabbed Brad's chair and shoved him back through the door and into the hallway. Brad struggled and tried to talk against the loose tape.

Spencer began to whistle.

They headed back to the elevator.

"Boy, if only Vanessa could see this, huh? Too bad you won't get a chance to say goodbye."

Spencer went back to whistling.

Then he stopped.

Why shouldn't she see this?

She had a hand in this. She should see what her actions have led to.

He spun Brad's chair around to face him.

"Where's your phone?"

On the floor by the elevators.

"That's right, thanks!"

Brad looked at him with a confused look. Spencer spun him back around and continued toward the elevators.

There, he picked up Brad's phone.

"Okay buddy, here's what we're gonna do. We're gonna call Vanessa. You're gonna tell her you need her down here. You need her to come down here right away. It's a... it's a matter of life and death, that sort of thing. Sound good?"

Brad nodded.

Spencer pulled the tape off again.

"Now, if you say anything other than what I told ya, things are gonna get ugly. Right?"

Brad nodded, a look of horror on his face.

Spencer looked at the phone.

It didn't make sense. It was just a screen. There were no numbers, no buttons, no... *wait.*

He pushed a button on the side and the screen lit up.

"Aha!"

He fiddled with it.

"How do you... how the hell does this work? Is this even a phone?"

Spencer looked up to Brad.

Brad was looking at the elevator.

Spencer looked there as well.

The number above the elevator door was changing.

7.

8.

Oh crap.

"Who's that, Brad? Did you forget to tell me someone was here?"

"No, no, I don't know who that is!"

Spencer grabbed the roll of duct tape he had dropped to the floor and hastily slapped a fresh strip over Brad's mouth.

He placed Brad out in the open, where someone would see him, then stood by the other side of the doors.

He watched the numbers change.

10.

11.

Brad was struggling again, trying to fight against the tape.

"Stay put, buddy. We'll get back to business soon."

13.

14.

Spencer could hear the car now, traveling up on its grinding cable.

Maybe it'll just keep going.

Yeah right. They're coming for you.

15.

16.

Spencer swallowed hard and tried to prepare.

The car came to stop.

Ding.

Ready to pounce, Spencer held his breath.

The doors opened.

Someone stepped out.

"Brad? What the..."

With a shout, Spencer slammed his fists into the intruders head.

The figure collapsed with a short cry.

Brad's head dropped.

Spencer was grinning.

I got this.

We got this.

Only then did he notice who was lying on the floor.

Oh shit.

Vanessa was sprawled out in an unflattering position. Spencer had a hard time seeing her like that. It was... unnatural.

Alright. Well, honestly, this works.

Yeah. Ends justify means and all that.

"Well look who joined the party, Brad!"

Brad screamed against his tape.

Spencer grabbed another rolling chair from a nearby office and got Vanessa in it. She was making soft, barely conscious noises as he taped her up in the same fashion he had Brad.

Then he squatted down in front of her.

God, she's still so beautiful.

His heart was pounding again.

She opened her eyes and looked around.

Spencer felt himself blush. He felt entirely naked, exposed under the beams of her gaze.

"What's going on? Who are you?" She asked blearily.

His heart sank. He had been scared of her recognizing him. Now, he was disappointed that she hadn't.

"You know me."

Vanessa saw Brad in his chair, looking at her over his bloody, taped mouth. She looked back at Spencer.

"I have no idea who you are. What is it you want?"

"No. You know me."

"I don't know you. Is it money?"

"Vanessa. Look at me. Remember."

She did look at him. He could feel her stare searching between the wrinkles in his sun-beat face, digging beneath the scraggly hairs sprouting from his face.

Then she laughed.

"Spencer? Haha, is that you?"

She's not afraid at all.

"Wow, I heard you weren't doing very well, but... wow," she said, still laughing.

Even now, she still mocks us.

"Stop laughing at me!"

"Oh Spencer, what do you think is going to happen here?"

Spencer ripped a big piece of tape and slapped it hastily over her mouth. She kept laughing into the tape.

Spencer grabbed his head in frustration.

We need a drink.

He stomped off down the hall to grab the bottle of Glenlivet.

Once back in the meeting room with the giant table and fully stocked liquor cabinet, Spencer drank most of the bottle in one long chugging pull.

He collapsed into the chair again in anger, frustration and sorrow.

So here we are... broken into a building we haven't worked at in years... two hostages taped to chairs in the hall by the elevator... what're we doing?

Let's just get out of here. We've made our point.

Spencer finished the bottle and tossed it aside. It didn't shatter as it hit the floor as he thought it would.

No. We haven't. She isn't sorry. She's laughing about destroying my entire life.

Spencer stumbled back over to the liquor cabinet. The bottles doubled in his swaying vision.

Let's see... what shall we sample next?

He pulled a bottle of Maker's Mark down and tore off the lid. He upended the bottle and chugged until it was gone. He tossed this bottle aside and gasped for breath.

He grabbed a bottle of something he could no longer read and staggered back out into the hall.

Brad was trying to inch his way toward the elevator's call button. Spencer watched, amused, as he leaned against the wall for support.

Brad looked like he was gonna try to push the button with his nose. Spencer didn't think he could bend over that far, but hurried down to stop him anyway. He almost fell over twice. He was burping up a lot of Maker's Mark.

He dropped the bottle he was carrying into Brad's lap, grabbed the back of his chair and hauled him away from the elevator.

"Woah there, buddy," Spencer slurred. He spun Brad's chair around and sent him wheeling down the hall. Spencer fell over once he lost contact with the chair.

He laughed, loud drunken roars, rolling around on his back. He finally got turned over and back on his feet.

Vanessa's eyes were giving him a stare of disdain, hatred, and most surprising to Spencer, simple annoyance.

He grabbed the back of her chair and threw her down the hall as well. Her chair crashed into Brad's, knocking him further down. Spencer skipped up behind them unsteadily, pushing their chairs back toward the meeting room.

"Time for a meeting, you two lovebirds," he said as he shoved them through the door.

Spencer kicked chairs out of the way and shoved the two of them up to the table.

He grabbed the bottle from Brad's lap and sat in a chair across from them.

This table made him powerful again. This table had intimidated people into signing things they shouldn't have. It was covered in the blood of people's dreams and futures.

"This table might look good covered in real blood."

He ran his fingertips along the table.

Did I say that out loud?

He looked over at the two and saw real fear in both their eyes.

Yep.

He cracked open the bottle and took a swig.

"So. How's it going, Vanessa? Brad and I were just getting caught up."

He took another drink.

"Me? Oh, I'm alright. I eat out of trash cans and dumpsters and sleep in alleyways. Last week, I even found a big box I could fit in for the night! So I can't complain, you know..."

He offered them the bottle. They stared at him over taped mouths.

"How rude of me. Let me help you guys."

Spencer stood up on wobbly legs and walked over to the liquor cabinet. He grabbed two glasses and set them on the long table. He poured booze into both, mostly on the table, and slid them down to the two. Then he finished the rest of the bottle.

He belched noisily and threw the bottle through the wall-sized picture window.

Glass exploded all over the office, raining down onto the street below. Spencer could hear it crash to the ground, people yelling up.

He leaned out the broken window and looked down. Tiny little people were looking up at him. Cars had pulled over. The broken glass was causing a commotion.

Whoops.

His hand slipped.

Spencer almost fell out the open hole, 17 floors down to the pavement below. He barely caught hold and dragged his weight back in.

Well that's pretty scary...

He looked back at Brad and Vanessa, who were both struggling to get out.

Pretty scary.

Spencer wheeled them both over to the open hole. They kicked and screamed into their tape.

Yes... getting good and scared now.

Spencer was laughing, a strange giggle he'd never heard before.

Vanessa was looking at him with pleading eyes.

"Yes? Have you got something to say?

She nodded quickly.

Spencer pulled the tape from her lips.

"Please don't do this. I had nothing to do with any of this, please believe me. It was all his fault. Punish him." She gestured toward Brad's furiously shaking head.

Spencer laughed.

"You two are great. Hilarious. Perfect for each other, really."

He ripped the tape from Brad's lips again.

In the distance, sirens started to wail.

"You bitch!" Brad screamed at Vanessa. "How dare you!"

"Brad, stop lying. Spencer, please believe me... he... he blackmailed me."

"Blackmailed you? You snuck into my office time after time while he was on the phone..."

"Shut up! Both of you!" Spencer grabbed Brad's chair and shoved him toward the hole. The wheels hit the edge of the wall and the chair leaned forward, his head and shoulders sticking out into the night air. He screamed.

The sirens grew louder.

"WAIT! DON'T!" Brad was screaming.

Half of Spencer wanted to push just a little harder, send Brad screaming out and eventually onto the side walk.

No, no. He's good and scared.

Spencer pulled back on the chair.

Cop cars pulled up at the base of the building. The commotion from the street was getting loud, even up here.

"Oh thank god!" Brad was babbling. "Thank god! Haha, I knew you weren't gonna kill me, I knew you were..."

Spencer's grip on the chair slipped, and he stumbled forward.

Brad fell forward through the open window, screaming. Spencer grabbed the chair in a mad scramble. Brad almost fell out.

Vanessa screamed behind him.

Spencer's head twisted toward her.

"What's your problem? Isn't this what you wanted? Brad to be punished?"

Vanessa shook her head.

"Please... just stop this..."

Spencer dragged Brad back in from the window ledge. Brad was sobbing.

Alright, they're really pretty scared. What are we doing here?

The sirens wailed from below.

Shit. How do we get out of this?

More police cars were pulling up.

Spencer was tired.

Exhausted, really.

What happened here? What have we done?

"Spencer... please just listen to me..." Vanessa was still babbling.

"Just... shut up."

It's done. I'm done. I'm not a cold-blooded killer.

What are we, then?

I'm... a corpse. A walking corpse. My life ended years ago, I just haven't caught up.

Maybe that's what this is all about. Maybe we really are done. Done trying to pretend I'm still alive.

Spencer leaned out the window.

This time he wasn't looking at the ground below.

He looked up at the stars in the black sky.

He breathed the cool night air in.

And he thought of something else he hadn't in years.

"How're the kids?" Spencer asked quietly. The sirens almost drowned the words out, but Vanessa heard.

"The kids? Our kids? I don't know. I guess fine, we haven't really talked in a while. They're busy, I'm busy, you know..."

Spencer nodded.

We really were awful people.

"Tell them... I don't know. Tell them I'm sorry, I guess."

And with that, Spencer Mills stepped out of the window, and into the night.

The air was refreshing as it rushed past his face.

He closed his eyes and smiled.

The world went silent.

END

Bonus story:

CHAPTER ONE

"Good day Mr. Stevens, I hope you enjoyed the service and thank you for coming."

As usual, the man walked past the girl without a word, his heavy gumboots thudding on the wooden porch and down the steps of the white-painted church. Abigail sighed. She wanted to be the best Christian she could be, just like her Daddy, but sometimes people made it hard. She watched as the man reached her father and stopped to accept the offered handshake.

"Nice to see you, Willem, always glad when you can make it," she heard her father say.

"Good service, Harlon," was the gruff reply before the man walked off.

Abigail was always surprised when anyone but Mama called her father by his first name. At this church high on the hill on the outskirts of the town, the only one for at least a sixty-mile radius, he served as both pastor and preacher, and that was how his congregation addressed him, even in daily life in the town. As her Mama stepped out from the cool of the church into the stifling Southern heat, she knew that her self-imposed duty had been completed; Mr. Stevens had been the last to leave. No one had asked eleven-year-old Abigail to take up a position welcoming and saying goodbye to the parishioners but as a child, she had watched her father stand at the bottom of the rickety old steps and do that very thing, while her Mama did the same at the back of the pews, just inside the wide, double doors. When she was eight, she had decided she should join in and took up a place on the porch at the top of the steps to do the same. Everyone had seemed to think it was sweet, and made the time to shake her hand and chat, except for Mr. Stevens. Then again, he didn't talk to anyone at all except for her Daddy.

Her Mama placed a gentle hand on her shoulder. "Good job, Abigail. Why don't you run and play with the other kids while Daddy and I finish up here."

Abigail skipped off happily, joining the group of town kids gathered in the church grounds. They were a mixed bunch, ranging in ages from eight to fifteen. The younger kids were playing closer to the church building, the older ones hanging out as far away as they could, too cool to be seen with Abigail's group.

"I see 'ol Kill 'em Scare 'em ignored everyone again," one of the older boys commented as Abigail joined them.

She frowned at him. "Hoyt, that name is not very nice, besides, it doesn't make a lick of sense, you can't scare somebody after you've killed them, silly."

"Wanna bet? He puts the willies up me and I bet he'd scare me even if I was cold in my grave."

Abigail turned to join her friends in watching the man walk away across the surrounding fields, heading for the woodland that indicated the beginning of the swampland. It was a long walk, and despite it being hotter than blue blazes, he was wearing the same thing he always did, a rough, brown woolen suit with the jacket buttoned tightly around him, heavy green gumboots and a flat cap that perched on top of his wild, unruly hair. His long, reddish beard streaked with grey and cold blue eyes finished off his look. She knew he looked a little frightening, but Daddy had always told her never to judge a book by its cover and to try to see what was on the inside. Mr. Stevens sure made that hard. Even in this town where people knew each other before they were born, he never spoke to a soul. Daddy had tried to invite him to occasions and family dinners, but he never came. He only came to town when he needed supplies, or occasionally appeared at the church on Sunday.

"He's just an old man who prefers his own company, you shouldn't be so mean, Hoyt Erwin," she said sternly.

"I don't believe it, I bet he's got dead bodies strung up everywhere, bleeding them out like an eight-point stag, getting' 'em ready to cure and eat."

Abigail laughed. "Don't be ridiculous! I swear; you'll go to hell for saying such things."

"If you're so sure, why don't we go and check his place out?"

"You mean spy on him?" Abigail's hand flew to her mouth, shocked at the thought.

"I mean, go and look around outside a little, check his place out, that's not spying. If you're so sure he's harmless, what's the problem?"

Abigail looked around the other kids frantically, hoping for back up. To her dismay, they were all nodding, agreeing with Hoyt.

"Yeah, Abigail, we'll only have a scout around. If we can't find nothing, then we'll agree with you and leave him alone."

"Sure we will, we promise."

The voices all came at her at once, confirming that they would stop their victimization of the man if she would only agree. She knew he had a hard time when he came to town, the local kids chanting names from a safe distance, or pelting his old, beat up truck with eggs as he drove away from the general store. The thought of being able to save him from that was tempting.

"So when would we go?" she asked, glancing around to ensure no one could overhear their conversation. Her Mama still stood talking to the two women who remained braving the heat under their wide brimmed hats. Her Daddy was nowhere in sight, probably back inside clearing up after the Sunday service.

"Tonight, after dark."

Abigail let out a squeak before she could stop herself. "You wanna go crawling around close to the swamp in the dark?"

"It has to be at night or else he'll see us and we'll all end up skinned alive with our throats slit. Besides, it has to be when we can sneak out and meet up. We don't want our folks asking a whole heap of questions about what we're up to."

Abigail felt fear fizzing in her tummy, making her feel sick. She didn't know what was worse, the spiders, cottonmouths and gators that inhabited the swamp or sneaking out of the house on her Mama and Daddy, and her the preacher's daughter! She wanted to tell them they were all crazy and to forget it, but she couldn't pass up on her first chance to really help someone. She could make Mr. Stevens's life more pleasant if she could prove to the others that there was nothing to fear. It would be between her and God as no one could ever know, but it would be worth it. Maybe he would speak to her on Sundays if the other kids stopped being mean to him.

"What's the matter Abigail, you chicken?"

She shook her head, making up her mind. "No, I'll be there. What time are we going and how are we getting out there?"

"What time do everyone's folks go to bed?"

The kids carried on making their plans, firming up the details of their nighttime adventure in hushed voices. Once everything was settled, Hoyt was the one to make the announcement, glancing up at the sun.

"We'd better get on home before we're late for the Sunday roast. Don't want to raise any suspicions and get in trouble already. Besides, my belly thinks my throat's been cut."

The kids laughed and turned to walk down the hill back into town, while Abigail went back inside the church to see what she could do to help her Daddy.

Chapter Two

Apart from the rattling hum of the old, clapped out air conditioning, the house had been silent for an hour. Abigail slid out of bed, where she had lain fully dressed under the covers, having put her clothes on after her parents had tucked her in and kissed her goodnight. As the pastor's daughter, she wasn't expected to run wild with the other kids and didn't have much choice of play clothes. She had chosen the least fussy sundress she owned and paired it with a pair of flat, summer sandals. She really wanted the gumboots she wore for collecting the eggs from the henhouse, but they were placed by the back door. She would have to cross in front of her parents' bedroom along the creaky hall and back. It was too risky.

Hoping the air system would cover any small noises she might make, she slid her window open. Like most of the houses in the town, hers was a single story affair, the hallways narrow and the walls thin. She slid out the window and hung there for a second, hanging by her fingertips before finding the courage to let go and drop to the ground. The cicadas and bullfrogs were deafening, but she still worried the sound of her fall had alerted her folks. She crouched there, waiting for any indication that someone was moving inside the house. It remained dark and silent, so she got up and scurried through the darkness, trying to run without her sandals making slapping noises on the baked-hard, dirt road. She had no fear of the dark or of anyone or anything in this safe, familiar town, only of being caught. She could already picture the disappointment on her Daddy's face if her naughtiness were discovered.

It seemed a long way for her eleven-year-old legs and her heart pounded in her chest as she ran, expecting to hear the yell of an angry adult asking her exactly what she thought she was doing running around town in the dead of night. Finally, she reached the outer limits where she was to meet with the other five that were making up the scout party, all of them boys and all of them older than she was. They were already there, talking in quiet voices, giggling excitedly about this latest adventure. The three that were lucky enough to own bicycles had brought them along, leaving three to hitch a ride. Excited at their bravery and the freedom of being out of town with no supervision in the dead of night, they made their way up to the church on the high hill.

Hiding their bikes around the back so they wouldn't be spotted from the road by any curious late night traveler, they headed for the field. They weren't sure exactly where Mr. Stevens lived, all they could do was follow the direction they had seen him take on many Sundays and hope they got lucky. They stumbled and tripped their way across the fields in the dark, not daring to use their flashlight while they were exposed out here.

As they reached the edge of the tall trees, they hesitated, all unwilling to admit their fear to the others.

"Promise me again, if we do this, you'll leave the man alone from now on?"

"Yeah, yeah, whatever," Hoyt replied in a muttered voice, shushing Abigail with a hand. "His house could be anywhere amongst these trees. Keep it down."

"How exactly do you propose to find it, smarty pants?" Abigail asked, mimicking Hoyt's half whisper.

Hoyt shrugged. "Look for tracks maybe?"

Abigail said nothing. Sure, all the boys learned to hunt and trap with their daddies around here, but she had no idea if Hoyt was any good at spotting and following a trail. She shivered, although not from the cold. The nights were as balmy and clammy as the days, and this close to the swamp, the humidity was even worse.

"I'm scared," she admitted to the others.

"What's wrong, don't want to meet your harmless old man in the dark?" Hoyt sneered.

"No, I'm scared we'll get caught and get into trouble. I'm scared one of us gets bit by a snake, or drowns in the swamp, or eaten by a gator."

"We ain't gonna get caught and as for the rest, you'll be fine. You got God on your side dontcha?"

Abigail flushed as the others laughed at her. As the preacher's daughter, she was often the butt of jokes or teasing from the others. No one around here asked *if* you went to church, they asked *where* you went to church, but being related to the pastor carried that extra stigma, giving them enough ammunition to make her their victim. Despite her daddy's reassurance that they would grow out of it and they didn't mean anything by it, it still hurt. Abigail bit her lip, thinking this whole idea was dumber than a box of rocks and she couldn't believe she had let herself be dragged into it.

"Come on, I think I can make out a small path through the woods."

Hoyt and the rest of the group moved forward, leaving Abigail no choice but to follow, or be left behind. Having no desire to be alone, she brought up the rear, keeping close. Hoyt used his flashlight, keeping it low to the ground and cupping his hand over the beam so the light didn't travel. Abigail's heart pounded in her chest and she was sure it was loud enough to alert every predator in the vicinity. Her mouth felt dry and her breathing was ragged, but she bravely carried on, trying to hold onto the good deed part of this nightmare.

They all came to a sudden halt as Hoyt held up a closed fist, indicating they should stop and stay quiet. He pointed at the ground, using the flashlight to highlight a thin line about three or four inches off the ground. It shone like spun silk in the torchlight and Abigail wasn't sure what she was looking at until Hoyt spoke in a low urgent whisper.

"We must be getting close. We have to be real careful, he could have trip wires all around this place. He might also have bear traps, pits and homemade land mines. Keep an eye out for any unusual mounds or piles of leaves and twigs, or any earth that looks freshly dug."

Abigail hadn't thought it would be possible to be more frightened than she already was, but the thought of her small leg being snapped at by huge metal jaws or falling into a deep pit with wooden spikes at the bottom turned her entire body to jelly. She knew enough from the boy's chatter to understand exactly what she might be facing.

"Just stay behind me and try to follow my footsteps if you don't know what to look for," Hoyt added, looking pointedly at Abigail. She gulped and nodded, taking up her place directly behind him, trying to emulate his long stride as they moved on.

Hoyt stopped once again and before Abigail's eyes could discern that they had reached the final tree line before a natural clearing, her nose burned with the most awful smell. It turned her stomach and she had to place a hand firmly over her mouth to try to control the automatic reaction of her stomach muscles, which were attempting to forcefully expel their contents. The only time she had smelt anything so bad was when she had come across some old, rotten, maggot-ridden road kill festering in the summer heat one day while walking home from church.

Hoyt snapped off the flashlight after placing a finger to his lips, silently telling them all to be quiet. They stood still, allowing their eyes to become accustomed again to the night sky. In the gloom, they saw Hoyt motion them forward and point. Taking up a safe place behind one of the tall, skinny trees, Abigail said a quick prayer before peeking round to see what the clearing held.

The moonlight and stars managed to light up the clearing much more effectively than the dense forest they had just passed through. It should have been beautiful, but it wasn't. The shack was ramshackle to say the least, the place lopsided and uncared for, several of the planks on the porch and steps rotted away, like a gap-toothed old hag. There were no windows, only black plastic sheeting roughly taped over the gaps where windows should have been. The screen door was open, hanging at a strange angle, the mesh torn and tattered. A few outbuildings dotted the place, in as bad a condition as the house. Abigail instantly felt sorry for the occupant, probably having to live this way due to lack of money. Her sympathy soon faded as she really took in the outside, the part her brain had been subconsciously avoiding.

Dead animals were hung around the whole place, their heads hanging, throats slit open to allow their blood to drain into rusty metal pails and plastic buckets placed below. Some were hung from the tree branches that encroached onto the clearing, while others were on poles and lines that looked like they might have been erected for laundry, but had a far more sinister load hung upon them now. She could make out several small animals, raccoons, muskrat, mink, skunks, rabbits; there were also foxes and surprisingly, coyotes and bobcats. Another line held what looked like eels. Abigail vaguely recalled hearing that eel blood was toxic to humans, why would he want to catch that in a pail? There were also a multitude of snakes, but she couldn't discern their type in the moonlight alone, not from this distance. The whole scene was eerily close to Hoyt's words that afternoon. He had been too close to the mark for Abigail's liking. What really shocked her was what hung from the strongest branches. There were several bears, and several gators. What manner of man could trap and kill these things so easily? Bears were normally shy and rarely spotted, and extremely dangerous when cornered. How did he have so many and why was he letting them hang out here and rot instead of using the meat for food and the fur for trade? There was no doubt that the crawling flesh was responsible for the horrendous stench that surrounded the place. Even in the moonlight she could see the white heaving that was the thousands of maggots that inhabited his macabre collection, and despite it being night, the flies buzzed around thick and fast.

She barely had time to take in the strangeness of it all or even properly form all the buzzing questions in her head before Hoyt poked her, an 'are you satisfied' expression on his face. Abigail nodded, then shrugged, then shook her head. This didn't mean the man was evil, just a little odd, and they had known that already. Illegal hunting wasn't exactly unheard of in these parts and she would bet that every family had done it at some time. Hoyt rolled his eyes at her, the whites of them gleaming in the dark. He leaned in close to her ear.

"If you still don't believe me then we're going to have to check out the outbuildings."

Abigail had no time to answer as the door of the shack flew open and Mr. Stevens stepped out. He walked to the edge of his rotten porch, stopping at the top of his steps. He lifted his nose high in the air and inhaled deeply, his head whirling round to the tress where they hid. Abigail couldn't help but let out a gasp. His face was wild, his eyes feral and movements animalistic as he jumped down the steps and landed on the ground.

"I smell blood," the wild man grinned. "Fresh, young, sweet blood. Has someone come to give me a donation?"

He chuckled then, the sound low and ominous, almost a growl in his throat. He snapped something between his hands and Abigail saw it was a length of the same type of thin, strong material that had made up what Hoyt had called a trip wire. Images of the open throats of the hanging, helpless animals and their staring, lifeless eyes filled Abigail's mind and she froze, the very blood in her veins turning to ice. Stevens took a step towards them and Hoyt knew their position was already compromised.

"Run!" he screamed, his voice high pitched and girlish as it echoed through the trees and bounced back to their ears several times over.

It was enough to break Abigail from her immobile status and she turned and fled with the rest. It soon became apparent that she couldn't keep up. She was disadvantaged by being smaller and younger than they were, not to mention being a girl in a sundress and sandals. She stumbled and tripped her way back through the forest, watching the gap between her and her friends widen as they sprinted for their lives, their survival instincts flooding their brains and muscles.

Abigail was jerked to a halt and her mind panicked. *He's got me, oh my Lord, he's got me, I'm going to die!* She kept trying to run forward, her legs refusing to give in while her brain already had. A ripping sound filled the night and she shot forward again. Glancing back, she saw a piece of pale blue material hanging limply from a tree. *It was only a branch; her dress had been snagged on a branch.* She giggled then, the relief bordering on hysteria. Her fevered brain had no more thoughts as the world went black for Abigail Adams.

Chapter Three

"Morning honey, time to get ready for school."

Betsy Adams' voice died in her throat when she saw her daughter's empty bed. She smiled, thinking her daughter had already risen and would be out at the hens, collecting the eggs. Then she frowned, sure that she had seen Abi's gumboots still sitting by the back door where they were always placed, ready to slip on before leaving the house. She went to check, and sure enough, there they sat. She opened the back door and called for her daughter. There was no answer. Worried now, she went to fetch Harlon.

"Abigail isn't in her room," she told him, wringing her hands.

Her husband was sitting at the well-scrubbed kitchen table, drinking a mug of coffee from the pot that Betsy had prepared earlier. "She'll be out doing her chores already," he smiled easily.

"I called her and there was no answer, and her boots are still at the back door."

"Well, maybe she decided it was too hot for the boots, and you know the chickens kick up an almighty ruckus, she probably didn't hear you."

Betsy shook her head, unconvinced by her husband's reassurances. She had a nagging feeling in the pit of her stomach that something wasn't right. "I'm going outside to check."

Fifteen minutes later, she returned, her face even more worried than before. "She isn't out there, Harlon. I've checked everywhere."

Harlon laid down his second mug of coffee. "Betsy, she's a good girl, I'm sure there's a simple explanation. This is the last week of school before summer vacation, maybe she went in early for some field trip, or for some extra study before a final exam."

"If she was doing any of those things, she would have told me. Let me spell it out for you, her chores aren't done and her bed looks barely slept in. Something is wrong, I just know it."

"Okay, let me go and take a walk around, talk to the other parents, see if there was something going on this morning that we didn't know about, see if anyone knows anything."

"I'm coming with you."

"No, best you stay here. If something is wrong, someone needs to be able to get hold of us, right?"

Betsy nodded, knowing her husband didn't really believe anything sinister could befall his daughter in this quiet town where neighbors were lifelong friends and everyone looked out for one another. He expected her to walk in the door at any minute, having taken it upon herself to do some extra chore, like going to the store to collect his morning paper for him. The heavy weight in the pit of her stomach told her otherwise. Two hours later, he returned with less than encouraging news.

"No one has seen her since yesterday, and every other kid was in bed this morning where they were supposed to be. There were no extra curriculum activities planned, official or otherwise."

Unbeknown to the worried parents, the events of last night had ended in a pact for the rest involved. Only once the others had arrived back at the church and grabbed their bicycles had they realized that Abigail was missing. They had waited and waited, but no sign of her small frame had appeared out of the woods and into the open field.

"We should go back for her," James had declared.

The others had protested strongly, being too afraid to face the horrors that waited in the woods again. "It's too late, he'll already have her," Hoyt said miserably. "There's nothing we can do now. If we go back there, we'll all die."

"We have to go and get help then, raise the alarm."

"For what? For them to find her dead body hanging from a tree, her blood draining into a bucket! Or worse, he'll have cleared everything up and there'll be nothing to find. I'll get the whippin' of my life for being out here as it is. I'll be beaten to within an inch of my life if they think

I'm making up stories. Think about it, it's what he'll expect us to do. Do you want to be grounded all summer? Abigail is gone, and us tellin' can't do anything to change that."

"So you want us to walk away, go home and pretend this didn't happen?"

"That's exactly what I want us to do. If we tell, he'll come after us. If we keep schtum, he might realize we ain't gonna say a word before he gets the chance. It's our only hope. There ain't none of us old enough to leave and never come back. You want to spend the next few years afraid to be alone, looking over your shoulder?"

"We could get the police; he can't do anything to us if he's in jail."

"First of all, nobody is going to believe us, when do our folks ever take us seriously about anything? Secondly, I already told ya, he'll have everything cleared up and there won't be a shred of evidence left to back us up. Then we'll be goners for sure."

They nodded their heads, allowing Hoyt to talk them out of what they knew was right. They had sworn each other to absolute silence, promising that they would never speak of this night again. Even under the gentle manner and worried expression of their pastor, they had held true to their oath, claiming they hadn't seen Abigail since they had left the church the previous day.

***

The town put in their best efforts. Search parties were formed and every spare minute anyone had was devoted to searching for signs of the missing girl. Hunters went out with their best dogs, carrying items of her clothing so they could get a handle on her scent. They searched surrounding woodlands and dredged marshlands using long poles and flat-bottomed boats to navigate the murky waters. Posters were printed and plastered all over town. The nearest police force were contacted and details were taken and added to some database somewhere. There was some excitement when one of the dogs picked up a scent but it went cold in the woods. The nearest house was the shack that belonged to Mr. Stevens. As the search team approached, there was nothing to see except for a rundown homestead and a genuinely concerned man who was sincerely apologetic that he couldn't help them. He had seen the girl at church on Sunday, but hadn't left his house since, and could think of no reason why she would be out in the woods close to his home. The hunters had searched for four more hours but the dogs hadn't managed to catch the scent again. Every effort turned out to be futile and gradually the search tailed off and people lost enthusiasm and hope. The town mourned and moved on.

As time passed, the posters grew faded from the sun, the paper drying out and becoming tattered, no one having the heart to take them down. The pastor kept up his good works, but there was a deep sadness within him during his sermons. His wife had aged terribly, deep worry lines etched into her face and her hair turning pure white. Everyone pitied them, while at the same time thanking the Lord that it hadn't been their child. There was much speculation about the fate of Abigail Adams, some saying she had just up and ran, rebelling against being the preacher's daughter. Others refuted that, saying she was too good a girl who loved her folks too much. There were theories of passing vagrants, coyotes and even alien abduction, but no one ever solved the mystery of Abigail's sudden disappearance. Life in the small town returned to normal. The others involved kept to their word, talking down any of them that might be close to breaking. It was too late to come clean now. As the years went by, they almost began to believe their own story, their conscious minds happy to put the bad memories away forever, as if they never happened. Deep in their hearts, they knew, but on the surface in their daily lives, they were as stumped as the rest of the town.

Ten years to the day had passed since the girl had last been seen when the church doors flew open in the middle of the sermon, and Preacher Adams' words faltered to a halt as Abigail Adams walked up the aisle and stopped dead in the middle of the church, staring at her father standing behind the pulpit.

Chapter Four

Every head had turned at the opening of the doors and as Abigail limped her way up the aisle, a collective gasp had rang out around the room. Some people let out a scream, others fled from their seats and out of the double doors, only to turn and watch anxiously from the porch, horrified yet too fascinated to leave. Abigail paid them no heed, she only silently observed her father. The preacher had dropped to his knees, ignoring the consternation of his flock as he thanked God above for the miraculous return of his daughter. Finishing his prayer with the most heartfelt Amen he had ever uttered, he flew towards his daughter, dropping once again to his knees in front of her, sheer joy shining from his eyes. He stroked her cheek.

"Abigail, is it really you? Oh my Abigail, you came home."

He swept her into a crushing hug, holding her tightly against him, tears of relief running down his face. The others who had been with Abigail on that fateful night glanced at each other, frantic and terrified that now their lies and deception would be revealed. Abigail's mother sat in the front pew, watching the scene with a hand over her mouth, her eyes wide, not quite sharing her husband's joy. For the most part, she wanted to fly to her daughter and hug her the way Harlon was hugging her, tell her how much she loved her and had missed her. The deeper, more primal part of her screamed at her that this was not her daughter, could not possibly be her daughter.

As the scene had time to sink in, more people left the church, some slowly, others running. Abigail's appearance was indeed disconcerting. She was filthy, with leaves and twigs embedded in her long hair, her nails were long and black, the pale blue color of her dress completely obscured by the dirt that coated it. She looked as if she had clawed her way out of her own grave, or the very pits of hell itself. However, the muck and grime and the sandals that had practically rotted away on her feet were not what frightened the witnesses to the miracle. Abigail Adams hadn't aged a single day in the ten years that she had been gone.

***

The town had no choice but to learn to accept this anomaly in their midst, as much as they didn't like it. After her parents had taken Abigail home, the townsfolk held a gathering on their own. They wanted to cast this creature out, not believing it could still be the same girl they had known and loved. However, Harlon Adams was their friend, their mentor, their shepherd. His delight, joy and firm belief that God had performed this miracle for him had been obvious. None of them could bring themselves to hurt him that way. The most sensible of the crowd managed to calm the outraged hotheads for the moment, telling them they should focus their attention on finding out what had befallen the girl first. They could take their anger and sense of injustice out on the perpetrator of this crime once they discovered the identity.

As the angry mob were settling into agreement, Betsy was sponging Abigail's filthy, skinny body in a hot bath. The girl hadn't uttered a word since her return, only staring at her parents, her face expressionless. Betsy could read nothing in those blank eyes. She felt nervous and unsure around the girl, but her mothering instinct had taken over. After the bath, she dried her gently with a fluffy towel, dressed her in what used to be her favorite nightgown and tucked her into bed. She only hesitated for a few seconds before bending to kiss the girl on the forehead.

The weeks went by, and still Abigail did not speak. She resumed her chores around the house, carrying them out efficiently but with none of the pride and eagerness she had previously shown. She would spend time with the family, helping her mother prepare the meals and eating at the table with them, accompanying her to the store and helping to carry the groceries, but there was none of the closeness they used to share. She went to church on Sunday, but did not resume her place on the porch to welcome the parishioners inside or thank them as they were leaving. She completed ignored the young men who, as boys, had abandoned her that night, and they finally began to relax again. They were making their place in this town, and didn't want it jeopardized. Hoyt was married, his first child on the way, his gun and ammo store thriving, the others at various stages of manhood, finding themselves and their place in life. They didn't speculate too much on what had happened to Abigail, concerned more for their own security. As long as she kept her mouth shut, everything would be fine.

Stevens hadn't come after them, hadn't even acknowledged them on his rare visits to town and church. They had decided that some sound or reflection must have given away their position, not some animalistic sixth sense as it had appeared in the heat and fear of the moment. He was just a man, and there was no way he could have made out their faces or identified them as they fled through the trees. The only fly in the ointment was Abigail herself, and that was turning out to be not so bad.

The small town doctor had recommended that Mr. and Mrs. Adams take Abigail to a specialist in the city for her speech. His check over had revealed nothing medically wrong, and no explanation for her lack of aging. He suggested to them that they not mention the circumstances to an outsider, for Abigail's sake. He felt that the silence was brought on by the trauma of what she had been through, and that the specialist would recommend therapy. It had gone exactly as he had said, but no amount of therapy and coaxing could make Abigail talk.

Harlon had never treated his daughter any differently and gradually, Betsy became used to this new and different Abigail, treating her much the same as before. They never pushed her to talk, but Harlon prayed for her emotional wellbeing continuously, wanting only her happiness. The only strange habit he had noticed was that every Sunday, she took a container and filled it with holy water from the font before crossing herself with the water, before and after the sermon. He never mentioned it to anyone, glad that his daughter had found something that comforted her. He had no idea that once he and his wife were asleep, Abigail would pour the water into a blessing bowl and carry it around the house, praying while she used the water to make the sign of the cross and other symbols on every access point to the house, no matter how small. Every door, window, vent and crack or gap was anointed with the holy water. Sometimes her tears dripped into the bowl, mingling with the blessed water, adding to its power.

Three months after her return, Stevens turned up to the church for the first time. Abigail was sitting quietly with her mother in the front pew, the congregation almost settled ready for the sermon to begin when the heavy boot falls were heard. Betsy felt Abigail tense beside her, and she took and squeezed her hand, wanting to reassure her daughter despite not knowing what was bothering her. Abigail pulled her hand from her mother's grasp and stood. Slowly, she turned, her face a mask of utter terror as she faced Stevens who was about to take a place at the end of a pew halfway down the church. Stevens's face turned ashen, his shock as he recognized the girl palpable. Events seemed to occur in slow motion as the members of the church watched Abigail raise an arm and point at Stevens. Her mouth opened wide, at first, silent and macabre, then suddenly, her throat broke free and released an ear-shattering scream that stunned the crowd. It was the first sound she had uttered since her return.

"Impossible," Stevens cried, his shock turning to rage. "You can't have got away!"

The man suddenly realized that all eyes were now turned to him, filled with anger and hostility. He had given himself away in his surprise. He turned and fled from the church. Men leapt up to follow, but others grabbed them.

"We know where he lives, let's go home and gather supplies first."

They watched as the man stumbled and lurched his way across the field in his heavy, awkward boots, fleeing for home. Betsy hugged a sobbing Abigail as the preacher tried to settle his flock, telling them it was not their place to exact revenge.

"What would you rather do, Preacher? Go to the police and tell them the story? Do you think they will believe you?"

"No, I suppose not," Harlon replied, pacing and rubbing his hands, knowing he had no real way of containing this crowd. "But he will receive his punishment eventually, be it in this life or the next. Higher powers will take care of that. We have no right to decide his fate."

"I'd say we have the right, you more than anyone. Just take a look at your daughter."

Harlon glanced at Abigail, the trembling, sobbing, hysterical, tiny form clinging to her mother breaking his heart and hardening his resolve. He turned and nodded.

"Everyone bring what you can and meet back here in fifteen minutes. Hoyt, will you open the store?"

Hoyt, fired up by the opportunity to take his revenge on the sick freak with the whole town behind him did more than agree. "I'll arm every one of you with the best I got, and for today, ammo is free."

The crowd cheered and made their way from the church, rushing down to the town for the chance to get their hands on their most coveted weapons, even if only for a day. Harlon made his way over to his wife and daughter. He stroked Abigail's hair gently.

"Was that the man who hurt you Abigail, the one that took you away?"

Abigail nodded, her deep, wracking sobs calming to mews and whimpers.

"Then God forgive me, but we're going to make sure he can't hurt you or anyone else again. You're going to be all right."

"You can't kill him, Daddy."

Harlon and Betsy shared a surprised glance and then nodded knowingly at each other. The therapist had said their only hope was that some trigger would free up the child's mental block, allowing her to talk. The trauma of seeing her abductor had been the required catalyst.

"I won't do it myself, but there is nothing I can do to stop the others, you saw them."

"No Daddy, you don't understand, you mustn't kill him."

"Hush now child, everything will be okay. I want you and your mother to stay here where you'll be safe."

With that, he left to gather his own weapons, crosses, holy water and his family bible that had been passed down through generations. By the time the lynch mob returned, he was ready to join them. Abigail and her mother watched as they made their way across the field, baying for blood. Once out of site, her mother closed the huge double doors and escorted Abigail back to the front pew.

Chapter Five

The most adept hunters had taken the lead, easily spotting and avoiding the booby traps set up around the clearing. They now circled it, closing in on the house, forming a tight ring with no weak points.

"Come on out and face us like a man, you sicko," Hoyt called. "I'm not a kid anymore, you don't frighten me."

A deep chuckle came from within the house, causing a few of the party to glance nervously at each other. Others were fuelled by the confirmation that their quarry was inside, a sitting duck. Their rush forward almost obscured the deep voice that came from the house, but not quite.

"Why don't you come in and get me?"

The horde barged inside, stopping in their tracks as they took in the scene before them. Inside, the room was bare, except for the walls holding inverted crosses and strange symbols painted on the walls, some bright red and fresh, others dried and flaking, the color of rust. Stevens stood in the center, a double circle filled with the same symbols drawn on the floor with the same bright red substance. Salt made up a third circle and goblets were placed at various point, the thickness of their contents and the metallic tang in the air leaving the vengeance seekers in no doubt that their contents was fresh blood.

"What the heck is this?" one man exploded as they piled into the room and spread out in a semi-circle.

"This is the devil's work," another cried. "He's in league with Satan!"

Others took up the cry; their outrage that evil had come to their god-fearing town rising to a fever pitch. How dare he taint their homes, their church, and their people! Hoyt raised his gun and the crowd silenced. Stevens laughed again, that deep chuckle that seemed to echo and resonate within the very marrow of their bones.

"Shoot him, Hoyt, take him down."

Hoyt fired the powerful, double barrel shotgun, his aim dead on, calm and steady.

Several people ducked as the bullets seemed to ricochet off an invisible force field and deflect to the side, exploding and shattering a huge hole in the rotten wall.

"What the ..." Hoyt exclaimed, knowing his aim had been bang to rights. He hadn't missed anything since he was a child.

"You can't break the circle," Stevens cried, almost dancing around with glee.

The crowd looked at each other, wondering if he spoke the truth.

"They can't, but I can," Harlon said quietly, stepping forward.

Stevens snorted. "You think your bible and cross can defeat me? How many times have I walked into your church, listened to your pathetic ramblings and walked away after shaking your hand? There is no power there."

"No, the power is in me."

Harlon placed his right hand on the bible and began to pray, the crowd's voices joining with him. Taking his bible, he swept at one of the goblets, sending it flying and spilling the contents. The other's watched Stevens's eyes grow wide with surprise then fear, as Harlon knelt and took out his holy water, throwing it forcefully across the floor. The salt hissed and fizzled, dissolving rapidly, the blood running and bleeding into itself, the clear lines washed away.

The circle was broken.

The gunfire was deafening as what seemed like a thousand shots rang out and barreled into Stevens, his body jerking and twisting around in a hellish dance of death as he was ripped apart by the close range fire. Finally, the frenzy died and the ringing in their ears subsided. They looked at the ravaged body that now lay at the back of the room.

"What now?"

"Take him outside; string him up like everything else out there."

"Throw him in the bayou, let him feed the gators."

The suggestions came thick and fast, the bloodlust not quite satisfied. Harlon shook his head, saying a prayer for forgiveness for each and every one of them, himself included.

"Look," came a startled cry.

Everyone turned to where the man pointed, focusing their attention on the center of the circle where a strange mist had begun to swirl and rise. Impossible wind rose and ruffled their hair as the mist swirled faster and higher. As it cleared, the figure of man appeared before them. At least, it looked like a man at first glance. On closer inspection, his ears were slightly pointed; his eyes were pitch; bottomless pits of emptiness. When he smiled at them, his mouth was filled with a terrifying amount of razor sharp teeth.

"You should have closed the portal first, preacher man," the thing said pleasantly. "Anyway, thank you. The soul that bound me is in hell where he belongs, waiting my return. Oh, what fun we're going to have when I get back! You have no idea how long I have been a servant to that miserable excuse for a human, now he's my slave forever. After all, a bargain is a bargain."

"Are you the devil?" Harlon asked in a whisper.

"As if that sniveling wretch would have the power to summon the master himself," the thing snorted, his face still pleasant but the cold, dead eyes revealing its true nature. "Now, since you so kindly broke the circle before closing the portal, there is the small matter of my other servant. How it managed to escape I'll never know, that fool could never do anything right. I have to admit I'd grown rather fond of it, and I want it back."

Before the group could react, the man-like thing stepped over the bleeding lines and disappeared outside. They gave chase but when they got outside, there was no sign of him anywhere. They couldn't locate a single track or footprint, and they resigned themselves to being defeated. They split into groups, some helping Harlon pray over the area and scrub away every speck of blood from the wooden floor while others dragged

Stevens's body to the edge of the bayou and dumped it in. After setting fire to the house and watching it burn to the ground, they made their way back to the church, where they found Betsy, alone and weeping, hysterically clutching at the empty space where her daughter had been.